Dedicated to my Grandpa Peng who taught me
everything lovely in life starts with respect for animals.

獻給我思念的外公
是他教我生命的一切真善美
始於對動物的尊重

Jenny W. Hsu

Author 作者
許維恕 Jenny W. Hsu

Translator 譯者
Simone Chang 張芷珩

Illustrator 繪者
Tara Mao 毛采薇

推薦序 Recommandation

《比莉》是一個美麗的故事，講述了一隻狗和她的救援者之間的情感。珍妮給了比莉她的關愛與慈心，而比莉則回以無條件的愛與動人的忠誠。在 PACK，這樣的幸福結局並不罕見。

庇護所自 2013 創立至今，我們見證了數百個人與家庭的故事。當收養者打開心門歡迎狗狗成為家中的一份子時，他們的生活也獲得了超出預期的陽光與歡樂。

一開始總是人想給狗狗一個新生活，但結局卻總是狗狗帶給收養者無限的快樂、愛與感恩之情。希望多些人能給收容所的狗狗們一個機會。或許很快的，你也將擁有你自己版本的比莉故事。

Larry Chi，社團法人台灣巴克動物懷善救援協會執行長

"Billie is a beautiful story of the special bond between a dog and her rescuer Jenny. By showering Billie with compassion and kindness, Billie reciprocated by giving Jenny unconditional love and unwavering loyalty. Here at PACK, we are all too familiar with happy endings like this.

Since the sanctuary's establishment in 2013, we have witnessed hundreds of individuals and families whose lives received an extra shot of sunshine and joy when they welcomed an adopted dog into their homes.

It always starts with the adopters wanting to give the dog a new lease on life, but almost without fail, it is the adopters whose hearts get filled with love and gratitude. Please give shelter dogs a chance and very soon, you will be sharing your own Billie story."

Larry Chi, Executive Director of PACK Taiwan

給 To：_____

The nights were cold, and the wind was strong,
Billie wondered what she did wrong.
Whenever she wagged her tail and begged for love,
The man with crooked teeth and icy stare
Would hiss and yell, "Stupid dog, be gone!"

夜晚涼颼颼的，風呼呼的吹著，
比莉困惑的問自己：「我做錯了什麼？」
每當牠搖著尾巴，乞求一點愛時，
那牙齒歪斜，眼神冰冷的男人
就會嘶啞地吼叫：「你這隻笨狗，走開！」

Billie lived on a construction site in Hangzhou, you see.
A beautiful Chinese city with endless plantations of tea.

But Billie never got a chance to explore and roam,
Because the man had chained her to a tree and made it her home.

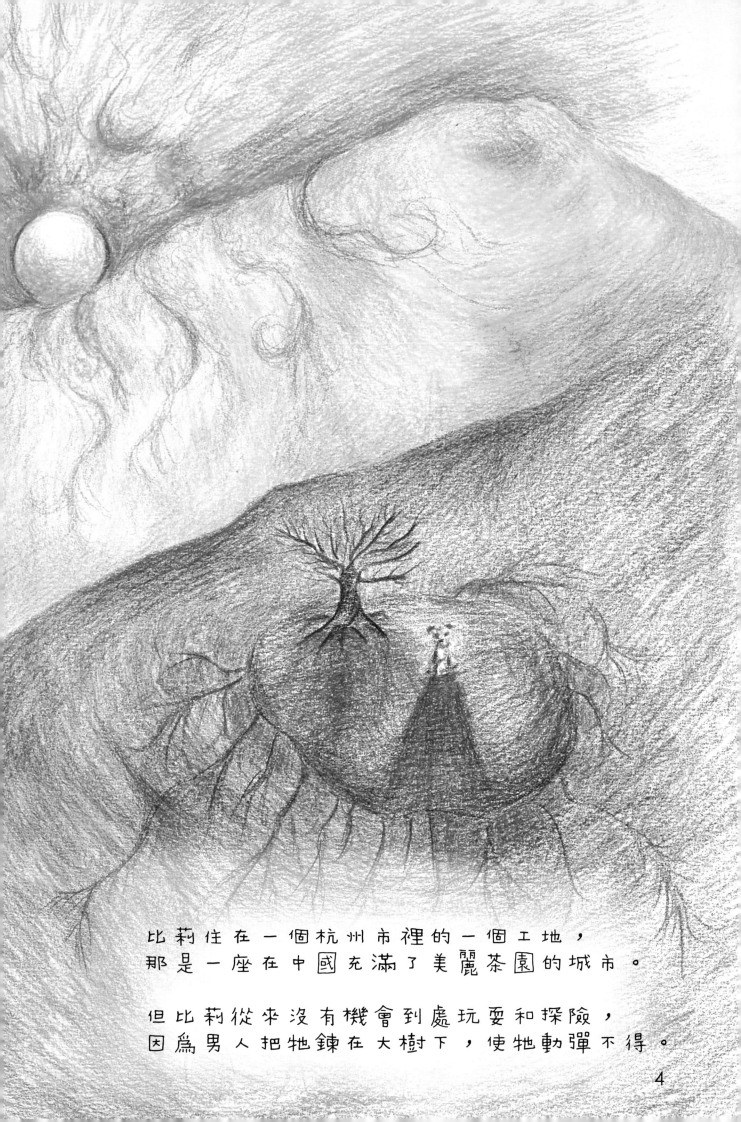

比莉住在一個杭州市裡的一個工地，
那是一座在中國充滿了美麗茶園的城市。

但比莉從來沒有機會到處玩耍和探險，
因為男人把牠鍊在大樹下，使牠動彈不得。

What the man didn't know was Billie had a secret friend,
A girl with golden hair, big smiles and gentle hands.
She visited Billie often and hugged her tight.
Whenever she visited, Billie would bark in joyous delight!

5

男人卻不知道，原來比莉有位秘密朋友。
是一位有著陽光般的笑容與溫柔小手的金髮女孩。

她常來看比莉，都會把牠牢牢的抱緊。
每次比莉都會開心地叫個不停！

One morning the man with crooked teeth and icy stare
Tossed in Billie's bowl smelly moldy noodles with fuzzy hair.

Billie sniffed the noodles and quickly turned her nose way,
That's when the man **screamed and punched** his fist in the air.

一天早上，
那牙齒歪斜，眼神冰冷的男人
把一坨發黴的酸臭麵條丟進了比莉的碗裡。

比莉聞了聞，立刻把鼻子轉開，
這舉動激怒了男人，
他氣到在空中揮舞著他的拳頭。

"You better not disobey me;
oh don't you dare!"

The man yelled so loud, poor Billie got very scared!

「你最好不要違抗我喔，
不然，我一定給你好看！」

男人大聲地罵喊，
可憐的比莉嚇壞了！

Billie tried to run away but she was chained to a tree,
She yelped, cried and tried to say sorry.

比莉試著逃走，但被鍊在樹下，牠叫著，哭著，試著道歉求饒。

The man got angrier each time Billie begged,
He got so mad that he **kicked** Billie's right hind leg.

13

比莉越哀求，男人就越激怒，
最後他氣到狠狠踹了比莉的右後腿。

When the man knocked Billie to the cold concrete ground,

Her body trembled with pain,

but her spirit wasn't down.

Billie just sat there quietly and remained a courageous pup,

Because she knew her special friend would come to scoop her up.

男人把比莉打趴在冰冷的水泥地上，
比莉的身體痛到不停顫抖，
但牠並沒有陷入絕望。

比莉靜靜地坐著，
心中依舊充滿了勇氣。

因為牠知道，
那位秘密朋友會來找牠，
把牠抱入懷裡疼惜牠。

Billie waited and waited and waited all day.

Then in the afternoon, her special friend came to play!

比莉等了又等，等了又等，等了一整天

直到下午，牠的秘密朋友真的來找牠了！

"Oh no, what happened to your leg, my Billie dear?

"We must take you to the vet soon, don't you fear!"

「噢，親愛的比莉寶貝，你的腿怎麼了？」

「別害怕，我們馬上帶你去看醫生！」

That night the girl with golden hair came with Jenny,
her dog-loving friend.

The two told the man Billie's time on the construction site
has come to an end.

They untied Billie from the tree and quickly took her away,

And that's how Billie's new life began.

那天晚上，
金髮女孩和她的愛狗好朋友，珍妮，
一起來看比莉。

兩人嚴厲地對那男人說：

「比莉不會繼續留在工地受苦了！」

她們將比莉從樹幹解開，
迅速帶著牠離開。

就這樣，
比莉的生命有了全新的開始。

In Jenny's arms
Billie felt so safe and pampered.
Although her leg was painful,
she never whimpered.

27

在珍妮的懷抱裡，
比莉感到安全又受寵。
雖然牠的腿非常痛，
但卻從未抱怨過。

The vet patiently examined Billie's broken leg,
And said, "no worries, we can fix her leg in a couple of days!"

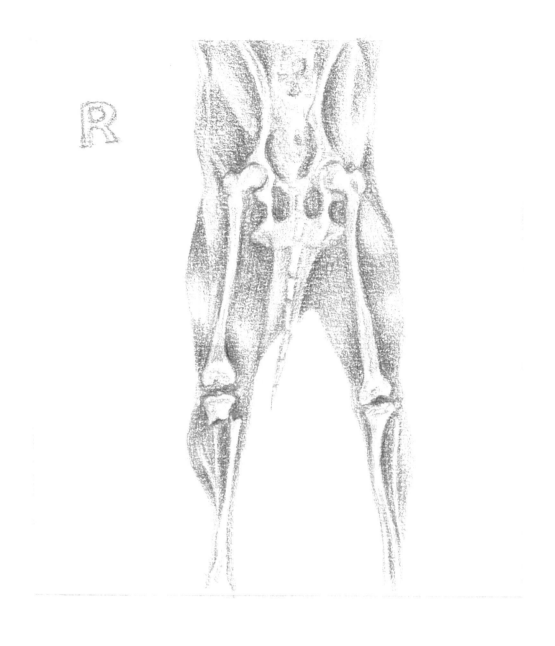

獸醫師耐心地檢查被踢到骨折的腿，

然後說：

「別擔心，我們很快就能治好比莉的腿！」

Jenny visited Billie at the vet every night,
She brought Billie yummy treats and made her feel alright.

Billie quickly became healthy and strong.
Her terrible days on the construction site were long gone!

珍妮每晚都去醫院探望比莉，
她總會帶好吃的零食給比莉，讓牠開心。

比莉變得健康又強壯。
牠在工地那段可怕時光，再也不會重演了。

"Billie is ready to go home," the vet said one day.
Jenny was so thrilled that she went to the clinic straight away.

33

有天獸醫師說：
「比莉可以回家了。」
珍妮欣喜若狂，
快馬加鞭地趕到獸醫院。

Jenny kissed and hugged Billie so very tight,
Promised she would love and protect Billie with all of her might.

What Jenny didn't know was Billie also made the same pledge,
That she would guard Jenny's heart like a brave loyal knight.

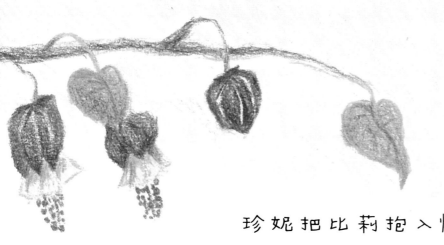

珍妮把比莉抱入懷裡，
親吻了牠的臉，
珍妮答應比莉，
一定會全心全意愛牠和保護牠

但珍妮卻不知道，
其實比莉也在心中許下了同樣的承諾，
自己一定要像一位勇敢的騎士，
忠心的守護著珍妮。

Billie's new home was full of laughter and joy
With two cats, a soft bed and boxes of toys.

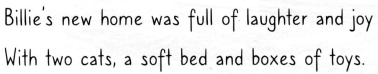

比莉的新家充滿了喜悅與歡笑，
這裡有兩隻貓，
軟軟的床和一箱箱的玩具。

Jenny took Billie on walks every morning and night.
Together they were each other's best allies.

珍妮每天早晚都會帶比莉出去散步。
她們是彼此最好的夥伴。

One day Jenny came home with tears in her eyes,
She felt so unworthy and completely broken inside.

有一天，珍妮含著眼淚回家，
她感到徹底心碎，
甚至懷疑自己的價值。

Billie sensed Jenny was feeling sad and blue,

Right away, she knew exactly what to do.

當比莉察覺到珍妮的傷心和低落時，
牠立刻知道該怎麼做。

Billie hopped on Jenny's laps and kissed her face,

Licked away the tears and nestled in her warm embrace.

Billie stayed by Jenny's side night after night,

Gave Jenny lots kisses whenever she cried.

Jenny put Billie's little paw over her heart,

And prayed that she would have the courage

to be strong no matter how hard.

比莉躍上珍妮的大腿，吻遍她的臉頰，
舔去珍妮的淚水，依偎在她溫暖的懷抱中。
比莉每夜都在珍妮身旁，
只要珍妮一流淚，比莉就會親她。

珍妮把比莉的小狗掌放在她的胸口上，
默默的祈禱，不管再難，
她都會有足夠的勇氣堅持下去。

It turns out that Jenny had
fallen in love with a man.
Who never bothered to include
her in his life plan.

Jenny thought it meant she wasn't
pretty, smart and good enough,

Because her affection for him was constantly rebuffed.

原來，珍妮愛上了一個人，
但他從未把珍妮 放在心上。

珍妮以為 是因為她不夠漂亮，
不夠聰明 ，不夠好，

這男人才會不斷的拒絕她。

Billie knew Jenny was sad, but wrong,
She was a wonderful loving woman with powers so strong.

"Jenny must love herself much MUCH more," Billie thought.
"I will love her until she realizes she has been amazing all along."

比莉感受到珍妮的痛，
但也知道她的想法是錯的，
珍妮是一個善良感性，
有情有愛、內心強大的好女孩。

「珍妮必須要更愛自己，」
比莉心想。

「我會好好愛她，
直到她知道她到底有多美好。」

Each day Billie did silly things to make Jenny smile.

Followed her around in the house like an adoring child.

比莉每天都做些可愛的傻事來逗珍妮開心。
牠就像個被寵愛的跟屁蟲，
到哪裡都要黏在珍妮身邊。

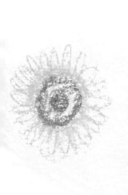

Weeks and months went by Jenny's shattered heart began to heal,
As Billie helped Jenny realize that her inner power was real.

一 日 過 一 日 ，

珍 妮 破 碎 的 心 開 始 慢 慢 癒 合 了 。

在 比 莉 的 幫 助 下 ，

珍 妮 也 意 識 到 她 內 心 的 確 有 股 強 大 的 力 量 。

One day Jenny woke up feeling something differently.
The wound in her heart was not so painful, finally.

She thanked her family, her friends and Billie,
For being so supportive and caring for her so lovingly.

有一天，珍妮起床時，心中有了不同的感受。

終於，她心裡的傷口不再那麼痛了。

她感謝她的家人、她的朋友，

還有比莉。

感謝他們一直愛她，支持她和關心她

Jenny leaned over,
scooped up Billie and kissed her nose,

"Thank you for loving me
even though I was so morose."

珍妮彎下腰把比莉抱了起來，
親吻了牠的鼻子，
「謝謝你在我低落時給了我源源不絕的愛。」

"I may have rescued you and untied you from the tree,
But it is **YOU** who saved me and set me free."

61

「雖然我救了你，把你從大樹解開
但是你卻用愛救了我，
因為你，我才能如此輕鬆自在。」

創作者介紹

Author 作者
Jenny W. Hsu 許維恕

Jenny was a reporter for over 10 years at various outlets including the Taipei Times, Central News Agency and the Wall Street Journal in Taiwan and Hong Kong. She has a masters in Special Ed from New York University and was a teacher for children with autism for five years. As a lifelong animal lover and advocate, Jenny has helped rescue dozens of dogs and cats. Born in Taiwan, raised in California, and she now lives in Taipei with her two rescue cats - Hannah and Scoops. Billie the Healing Dog is her first book.

前華爾街日報駐台和駐香港記者，也曾在中央社和Taipei Times任職過。是紐約大學特殊兒童教育碩士。曾於紐約市擔任自閉症特教老師五年。生於台灣，長於美國，目前居住在台北，並有兩隻前浪貓室友——許漢娜＆許獨家。Jenny一直都非常支持並投入動物救援。
《Billie》是她第一本書。

Translator 譯者
Simone Chang 張芷珩

Simone is a senior at Taipei First Girls High School with a deep affection for cats and dogs. In this book, she wishes to underscore the bond between animals and humans. She founded PrinceE, a non-profit animal welfare organization consisting of high school students with the mission of teaching students in rural areas of Taiwan about animal welfare. Currently, she is an intern at a veterinarian office.

就讀市立北一女中三年級，愛狗成痴、惜貓如奴。Simone十分重視動物福利，號召了一群高中生組成了學生組織PrinceE，致力將動保知識帶入偏鄉小學。現擔任獸醫師志願助理。

Illustrator 繪者
Tara Mao 毛采薇

As an illustrator, Tara combines her love for nature and animals with her passion for art. She believes in the healing power of images. Tara wishes to dedicate Billie to all the animals around us and thank them for giving us pure unadulterated love and keeping us company through all the dark times.

Tara喜愛自然、藝術與動物，尤其喜歡畫狗狗和貓咪，希望能透過圖像傳遞治癒的力量。這次她希望藉由繪製比莉的故事，來謝謝這些毛小孩們，在生活中給予我們最純淨且無條件的愛，陪伴我們渡過那些曾經黑暗荒蕪的歲月時光。

比莉完成腿部的手術後，
珍妮去醫院接牠。除了腿
傷，當時的比莉也有嚴重
的皮膚病，導致身體有好
幾處部位掉毛，包括牠的
額頭。

Jenny picks up Billie from the
hospital after her leg surgery. Apart
from a broken leg,

Billie also suffered from serious skin infection which caused her to lose hair
all over her body, including her forehead.

經過幾個禮拜的休養，
比莉變成一隻愛玩並充滿自信的狗。

After several weeks of recovery,
Billie transformed into a playful dog full of confidence.

有彩蛋！
To be continued...

想一想，聊一聊 Think & Share

Do you have any animals in your life? Who are they?
你生命中有任何動物嗎？牠們叫什麼名字？

What do you like or dislike about animals?
你喜歡動物嗎？為什麼？

How should we best take care of the animals in our lives?
我們應該如何好好照顧我們生命中的動物？

Billie's first owner was mean to her. What do you think is the best thing to do when we see animals being mistreated?
比莉一開始沒有被好好的照顧。
當我們看到動物被虐待，我們應該怎麼做？

The blonde-haired girl and Jenny rescued Billie together. Did you and your good friend ever accomplish a difficult task together?
金髮女孩跟珍妮一起去救比莉。
你是否曾經跟好朋友一起完成一件困難的事？

Jenny really liked a boy but he didn't like her back. Have you been rejected by a friend before? How did it make you feel?
珍妮很喜歡的男生並沒有喜歡她。你曾經被一個你喜歡的人拒絕嗎？
當時你的感受如何？

What do you think is the best thing to do when we are rejected by someone we love?
當被一個人拒絕時，我們應該如何反應？

Jenny was sad because she didn't love herself very much. How do you feel about yourself?
珍妮一開始很難過因為她並沒有好好愛自己，你對你自己的看法是什麼？

What action can we take to love ourselves more?
我們能做什麼來多多愛自己？

What action can we take to love others more?
我們能做什麼來多多愛別人？

國家圖書館出版品預行編目（CIP）資料

比莉／許維恕（Jenny W.Hsu）作；毛采薇（Tara Mao) 繪；張芷珩（Simone Chang）譯.
-- 一版 .-- 臺北市 : 速熊文化有限公司 , 民 111.11
　70 面 ; 21x29.7 公分
譯自 : Billie.
ISBN:978-626-95037-3-5

863.599　　　　　　　　　　　　　　　　　　　　　　　111016568

書名：Billie 比莉
作者：Jenny W. Hsu 許維恕
譯者：Simone Chang 張芷珩
繪者：Tara Mao 毛采薇
出版者：速熊文化有限公司
地址：臺北市中正區忠孝東路一段 49 巷 17 號 3 樓
電話：(02)3393-2500
出版年月：112 年 1 月
版次：一版
定價：台幣 390
ISBN：978-626-95037-3-5
代理經銷：白象文化事業有限公司
401 台中市東區和平街 228 巷 44 號
電話：(04)2220-8589 傳真：(04)2220-8505
著作權管理資訊：如欲利用本書全部或部分內容者，須徵求著作產權人同意或書面授
權，請逕洽速熊文化有限公司